THE CURIOUS MOUNTAIN MAN

MOVIN' TO THE MOUNTAINS
BOOK 2

CASEY COX

ABOUT THE BOOK

I'm a nerdy, neurodivergent librarian who lives a quiet life in the mountains. While out birdwatching one day, I stumble upon a giant of a mountain man bathing in the lake.

Naked.

I manage to run away, hoping he didn't see me.

And then he shows up at my library.

Something about him lures me in. Sure, he's tall, bearded, and insanely gorgeous, but there's a gentle curiosity in his eyes. And when he looks at me, it's like he's trying to understand me...

Orrrr maybe I'm imagining it.

Yeah, that's probably it. I mean, why would a handsome, barrel-chested lumberjack like Branum be interested in a Mr. Plain and Boring like me?

1

Branum

My skin prickles... Eyes are on me.

I can *feel* it.

My survival instincts are well-honed.

A childhood spent on the run with a father hiding from the law, needing to keep a low profile, constantly keeping a lookout over my shoulder, has equipped me with a sixth sense for these things.

I kick off my hiking shoes and peel the shirt off my sweaty back, dropping it onto the jagged edge of a boulder.

Lifting my arms overhead for a much-needed stretch after a five-hour hike, I stare out at the river that runs through the back of my fifty-acre property.

I'm moving normally. Acting natural.

I'm not sensing danger, just...*a presence.*

And if someone has trespassed onto my land and is watching me, they're about to get more than they bargained for.

I unzip my shorts and push them down my legs and step out of them. Then I hook my thumbs into the waistband of my briefs and do the same.

I stand to full height, soaking in the rays as they stream down on my naked body.

I'm the middle child of three brothers, but I'm much larger than Harrick and Marsh. Running my timber yard not only keeps me plenty busy, it also means I'm in pretty decent shape. Good thing, too, because while my metabolism may be slowing down in my thirties, my appetite sure ain't.

I turn my head from side to side, slowly, like I'm simply taking in the rugged landscape and beautiful tall pine trees, not trying to clock from which direction I'm being spied on.

I click my jaw to clear my ears, on the hunt for any sound, any indication, to confirm I'm not alone.

Nothing.

But that doesn't mean there's no one here, it just means they're good at being stealthy.

I climb onto the giant boulder and curl my toes over the edge before I dive in. The cool blue water sets off a tingling sensation as it washes over my heated skin.

I love being in nature. Sky, water, mountains. The elements ground me and make me come alive at the same time, remind me of what's real. If it's an outdoor activity—hiking, swimming, fishing, you name it—I'm in.

I swim underwater for as long as I can hold my breath before bobbing to the surface. I flip onto my back and float for a while, gazing up at the endlessly blue sky.

The sun beats down on parts of my body that are breaching the surface of the water—my face, my toes, my shoulders, my cock.

I reach down and readjust my dick, resting it flat along my stomach.

It starts to thicken.

I'm not an exhibitionist by any means, but there's no harm in toying with my anonymous onlooker is there? If they don't like what they're seeing, they're free to leave and trespass on someone else's land whenever they want. No one's holding a gun to their head.

After all, *they're* invading *my* privacy.

I run my fingers along the underside of my exposed cock, and as it grows, it rises into the air. A droplet of pre-cum pearls at the slit.

I lift my head so that my ears are fully out of the water.

Still nothing but the sound of the river flowing and birds chirping.

And then... A crackle, like someone stepping on a twig or fallen branch.

My pulse accelerates, but I don't let it show.

It could be an animal, or if it is a human visitor, it's most likely a lost tourist. Even though I live on the outer edges of Thickehead, the charming mountain town attracts a swarm of year-round tourists to the region.

There's a hiking trail a few miles away from my property line. Maybe someone took a wrong turn?

I stop floating and stand in the waist-deep water, swiping my hands through my slick hair, brushing it off my face.

I make my way toward the water's edge, taking long, deep strides, letting my eyes roam through the thick forest, trying to catch a glimpse of whoever is there.

I haul myself up onto the giant rock I dove in from and pat myself dry with my T-shirt. I bend down to gather my clothes when I hear a sound to my right.

Footsteps.

Dropping everything, I race off in the direction of the sound. Yep, somebody is definitely on my property.

I give chase.

The thing about running barefoot in a forest is that it kills your feet. As keen as I am to find out who my intruder is, a few prickly twigs spike painfully into my soles, quickly putting an end to things.

Dammit. They're getting away.

I scan my surroundings, hoping to catch a glimpse of whoever it is. Suddenly, in the gap between two massive trees, a person comes into my line of sight.

They're hightailing it out of here as fast as they can, but for a few brief seconds, I get a clear, unobstructed view.

It's a man.

Wearing a navy blue shirt with a black backpack flung over his shoulders.

But it's not what he's wearing that captures my attention.

No.

The detail my eyes fixate on is the mop of red curls on top of his head.

I have my answer. I know who my unexpected guest is.

He slips out of view, but I stand there, grinning like an idiot.

A naked idiot.

But it looks like this naked idiot is about to pay a visit to the local library.

2

PJ

Five, six, seven, eight taps on the top left corner of the book with my left hand.

I then silently count out eight taps on the top right corner of the book with my right hand.

Good.

Things are even.

I'm...balanced.

"PJ."

My boss's voice startles me, even though it's barely more than a whisper.

I turn around from where I've been processing books and sorting them onto the returns trolley, organizing them by genre and author surname.

"What's up, Trevor?"

"Someone's just walked in. Can you please serve them? I've got to jump in for kids reading hour."

"Go and read to the children." I wave him off. "I'll take care of everything else."

Trevor sends me a grateful smile. "You're the best. Thanks, PJ."

"No problem."

Trevor takes off for the reading room in the corner of the small library, while I spin around and stride toward the counter.

I take exactly two steps before screeching to a standstill. My eyes widen, and my entire chest clenches.

There's a man standing at the counter.

Not just any man, though.

It's the same man I spotted in the woods yesterday, except this time, he's wearing clothes—a green flannel shirt over a black T-shirt, to be exact—which is a shame because he looked great naked. His golden skin glistened in the mid-afternoon sun, and his body looked like it belonged on the cover of one of the many, *many* romance novels I own. Solid. Rugged. Manly.

What is he doing here?

With my heart thundering in my chest, I approach the counter. I only saw him from a distance yesterday. Now, standing so close to him, I can make out the color of his dark eyes. They're fixed on me as I get closer.

I also notice how thick and luscious his brown hair is, and I glimpse the first few strands of gray starting to pepper his full, thick beard. Mmm, that's sexy.

Oh god, did he see me yesterday?

I hoped I'd managed to sneak off without him noticing, but what if he saw me? Am I in trouble? Did I do something wrong?

Or maybe it's purely a coincidence that he's showing up right now. Maybe he wants to, I don't know, borrow a book or something.

The powerful stare he's aiming my way makes me think that's unlikely.

I place my palms on the counter, inhale, and as I breathe out, I summon the strength to look up at him. Jesus, he's tall. I mean, everyone's tall compared to me, but he's got to be at least six-four, maybe more.

My eyes meet his. Turns out, I was wrong about their color. Yes, they're a dark chocolatey brown, but there are flecks of gray swirling in them, too.

They're beautiful.

He's beautiful.

And most likely pissed at me for spying on him, even though that wasn't my intention. I was on the lookout for a mountain bluebird, the hot-as-heck lumberjack I stumbled upon was a completely unexpected surprise.

A pleasant surprise, sure, but I don't go around peeping on naked guys. That's gross. I got a little lost and was trying to find my way back to the hiking trail.

I drop my hands to my thighs and tap each leg exactly five times.

I'm a librarian. I'm a professional. I can handle this.

I put on a bright smile. "Good morning. How may I help you?"

The giant mountain man stares at me for a few moments. "I'd like one...ticket, please."

His voice is as deep and thick as I may or may not have imagined it would be.

"One ticket for what?"

"Here. I'd like to...come in...here." He looks around the library.

I can't tell if he's having me on or not.

"You don't need to pay admission to come in," I tell him with a straight face, in case he's being serious. "This is a public space. Everyone is welcome."

"Okay." He glances around again. "And what, everyone's allowed to take whatever book they want?"

"*Borrow*. People can borrow books, and then they return them."

"And how do I borrow a book?"

You know what, I actually think he's being legit. He really doesn't know, and something about that is both charming and a little concerning at the same time.

But I won't judge him for it. Lord knows I've been on the receiving end of people's criticisms my whole life. It's a horrible feeling. I guess some people don't know the ins and outs of how public libraries work. That's nothing to be ashamed of.

"If you'd like to borrow books, I can sign you up so you become a member."

"I see. And how much is that?"

I smile because the cuteness is just too much. "Nothing. It's free."

"Okay. Let's do it. Sign me up..." His brown eyes drift to my name badge. "PJ."

I latch on to the countertop for support. My name has *never* sounded so sexy or so husky...ever.

I walk over to the computer, and he follows from the other side of the counter.

"All right, let's start with your personal details. Name?"

"Branum Grady Duncan."

I swallow a grin. Awww, he supplied his middle name.

I remain professional as I collect his remaining information, before explaining how things work and printing out his library card.

I manage to do a pretty good job of ignoring how deliciously attractive he is.

Full disclosure, I have a thing for mountain men. It's not the only reason why I moved to Thickehead, but I'm not going to deny that the thought of getting swept off my feet by one of the big, burly alpha mountain men I read about in my romance novels every night may have played some part.

Except, in the books I read, the character who the mountain man falls in love with isn't a nerdy ginger librarian with OCD, a passion for birdwatching, and a strong preference for staying at home curled up on the couch with a good book rather than doing anything involving people.

That said, as far as meet-cutes go, catching a glimpse of a handsome, barrel-chested, naked guy in the river ranks pretty highly.

But is it really a meet-cute if we didn't actually meet?

"Great. Thanks, PJ."

I'm snapped back to reality by Branum's deep voice. I look up at him and smile shyly. I must've reached the end of my new-member spiel. Okay, so maybe I haven't been doing as good a job as I thought I was at staying professional. But in my defense, how often does a romance-cover-model-worthy muscled mountain man swoop into my otherwise plain and boring existence?

Ne-ver.

Well, apart from yesterday at the river...

Oh, yeah, *that*.

Did Branum see me yesterday? Is that why he's here? Or is a man who thought he had to pay an admission fee to enter the library really here to borrow a book?

My smile fades as Branum just stands there, looking at me. He doesn't seem mad, more like he's, I don't know, curious.

Maybe I'm just being paranoid...

But then, why does he keep staring at me?

It can't be because he's attracted to me, that's for sure. Kids in high school took my initials and renamed me Plain Jane, because, well, I'm as plain as they come.

Except for the red hair, I guess.

And the freckly face.

And the mismatched eyes.

They're all things that make me stick out, but not in a good way. And personality-wise, there really is nothing that stands out about me, good, bad, or otherwise.

I clear my throat and stare into those deep dark eyes. "Is there anything else I can do for you?"

"No. You've been a big help. Thank you... *PJ*."

3

Branum

"Thanks for helping out with this," my younger brother Harrick says, handing me another massive cardboard box.

I make sure I've got a good grip on it before I take it from the bedroom downstairs into the living room to add it to the rest of the boxes we've been putting there all morning.

"Don't mention it," I mutter over my shoulder.

"He really is great," I overhear Eddie, my brother's boyfriend, say as I leave the room.

I smile to myself, happy that my brother has finally found someone. Marsh and I had been worried about him after he came back from serving. He was closed off. Reserved. Possibly even depressed. So unlike the talkative, annoying dipshit kid we grew up with and loved.

But the truth is, Harrick had been a changed man ever since circumstances tore him and Eddie apart eleven years ago, during the summer they first met. I'm glad fate—well, a rainstorm and some good timing—brought them back together.

Eddie's a great guy, and he's done the unthinkable—he's brought the old Harrick back from the dead. Guess love really is that powerful. Not that I know much about that. Fate hasn't blessed me in that area of my life.

I drop the box into the living room and swing around to go back for more when my mind revisits my trip to the library yesterday. I felt like such a damn fool, asking PJ those basic questions, but apart from a couple of times at school, I'd never set foot in a library before.

I only knew I'd find him there because I heard some people talking about my red-haired intruder arriving in Thickehead recently, and one of them mentioned he worked at the library.

PJ.

My smile grows.

What a cool name.

What an intriguing guy.

What a *sexy* guy.

His fiercely red curly hair framed his face and matched the freckles that dotted his nose and cheeks. He had the cutest button nose and sweet pink lips. And his eyes. I'd never seen eyes like that before. One light brown, the other a dazzling green.

Not to mention he was *tiny*. I could probably lift him up with one arm and throw him over my shoulder.

Fuck. Me.

I've never met anyone who's had that sort of an immediate effect on me, and I haven't been able to get PJ out of my head since the moment I left the library.

Harrick and Eddie meet me at the top of the stairs. Empty-handed.

"No more boxes?" I ask.

"Oh, there's plenty more," Eddie responds with a smile. "But I heard from a very reliable and incredibly attractive source that if I don't feed you every three hours, I may not make it through the day alive."

"Thanks for ratting me out." I grin at my brother. "What's your boyfriend going to think of me?"

"Only good things," Eddie assures me with a laugh. "Now come on. We've worked up an appetite, too. You like pancakes, Branum?"

My eyes light up. "Do I ever!"

Fifteen minutes later, the three of us are scoffing down what, for me, will be the first of at least three plates of pancakes at the Pancake Pantry. We came before the lunchtime rush so managed to score a corner booth.

"Eddie's received an offer on his father's house," Harrick tells me, glazing his pancakes in maple syrup. "That's why we're in such a rush to get everything out."

"That's great news," I say to Eddie. "You gonna take it?"

"Yeah. I think I will." He stops eating. "It's bringing up a whole bunch of emotions, being back there."

He turns to my brother, and Eddie's eyes start to well. I look over at Harrick, and damn, *his* eyes are turning glassy, too.

Man, this love thing is intense. Especially with their history.

I let them have their moment while I excuse myself and head back to the counter to order another plate of pancakes, this time chocolate. When I return, they're back to normal, but they're sitting closer to each other.

"Heard you were at the library yesterday," Harrick says with a shit-eating grin. "Gotta say, I was surprised... Didn't think you could read."

I flip him off and laugh.

Brotherly banter, even if he has no idea how close to the truth his words are.

No one does.

I've managed to hide it all my life. But when I was at the library yesterday, I noticed there was a group of young kids being read to.

I'd like to be able to do that myself one day.

Read.

Properly, that is.

I get by, barely. I don't want to break a sweat every time I open a freaking letter or come across a sign. Thankfully, I've got a secretary who takes care of all my comms for me, and like I said, I can read basic things, but it's not enough.

It's embarrassing to admit, but I'm lost.

I don't want to be lost anymore.

Harrick snaps his fingers in front of my face. "Earth to Branum."

"Sorry. Must've spaced out there for a moment."

"So, the library?" he picks up. "Why were you there? Did you need to take a piss or something?"

"No. I..."

My second plate arrives. "Thanks, Mrs. K."

"No problem. Enjoy, hun. Let me know if you need anything else."

"Thanks, I will."

She leaves, and I push the plate away, causing Harrick to narrow his eyes in suspicion. Yeah, me pushing food away is *that* unusual.

I'd been planning on telling my brothers soon anyway, but since I got busted at the library, it seems like a good time to tell one of them at least.

"I'm thinking of getting my GED," I announce, then explain to Eddie, "I dropped out of school early."

He gives a small nod. "How early?"

"Ninth grade."

Harrick's brow is furrowed, his jaw set tight. "Our fucking father."

"It's not his fault," I say, since I'm always the one who defends him. "Well, it's not *only* his fault."

Harrick stares at me intensely. "What's that supposed to mean?"

"It means..." I take a breath. "It means I can't read very well. I... I never learned. Not properly, anyway."

"Oh," they both say at the same time.

"Yeah. *Oh*. I've been thinking about this for a while, but I'd like to learn to read, and then I'd like to sit the GED."

"I see," Harrick says, taking it all in.

"Sorry if this is a stupid question or out of line, but you run a business, don't you?" Eddie asks.

"I run a timber yard. Not like I need a PhD for that. And like I said, I can read some. I'm also great at faking it, and I get help whenever it comes to anything complicated."

Harrick's intense eyes land on me. "Is that why you always come to me with contracts to review?"

I scratch the back of my neck. "Yeah."

He gives me a small nod. "If you want to get your GED and

learn to read, that's great, man. I fully support you, and if you need anything, I—"

"*We*," Eddie interjects, and Harrick smiles.

"If you need anything, we are both here for you."

"Thank you...both."

"And sorry about my stupid joke before," Harrick says. "I wouldn't have said it if I'd known."

"It's fine. No one knows."

"What about Marsh?"

I shake my head. "I'll tell him next."

"Right."

I look between them, then taking advantage of the lull in conversation, I pull my plate back and set about destroying the chocolate stack. It's only when I'm about halfway done that a thought occurs to me.

"Wait." I finish chewing. "How did you know I was at the library yesterday?"

"It's Thickehead," Harrick replies with a shrug. "Everyone knows everything around here. You take a big enough dump in the morning and by lunchtime, you're the talk of the town."

I look down at the gooey chocolatey mess on my plate and push it away again. "Thanks for that."

"There's a new librarian working there," Eddie supplies, smiling. "Think he might be gay, too."

"That so?"

"Yeah. I ran into him last week. He seems nice. I love his red hair. He struck me as...unique. But in a good way."

"In what way exactly?" I ask.

My brother shoots me a questioning look. "Why do you care?"

"Just curious."

"Right." Harrick smirks. "You wouldn't happen to have a thing for library boy, would you?"

"Fuck off." I turn back to Eddie. "Did he say anything else?"

"Not really. Only that he's new in town, and he asked about

good places for birdwatching. I suggested the hiking trail near your place actually."

"Huh."

So that explains how PJ ended up on my property. He must've wandered off the path.

Thank you, Universe.

"What's the guy's name?" Harrick asks Eddie.

"PJ," I reply, and my brother's face lights up like a freaking Christmas tree.

"He had a name badge on," I grumble in an attempt to defuse whatever scenario his pea brain is concocting.

"Sure he did. Oh, and looky here. Now that you'll be studying for your GED, I guess you'll need to spend a lot more time at the library...with PJ."

"Yeah." I drag the plate back and lick my lips. "I suppose I will."

4

PJ

"He's ba-ack," Trevor singsong whispers in my ear.

I close my eyes as a smile stretches my lips. There's only one person my boss can be referring to. The same person who's been stopping by the library every afternoon this week.

Branum Grady Duncan.

"I see. And you're telling me this because?"

Trevor rolls his eyes. "Oh, come on. Please tell me you're not really that clueless. You have to see it."

"See what?"

"The way that man stares at you. Seriously, I walk past where he's sitting just to make sure he's not pleasuring himself under the table."

"Sure. *That's* the reason."

"Ah-ha."

"Ah-ha, what?"

"So you admit he's good-looking?"

"I never said he wasn't." And hell, after seeing him naked, you'll never hear me say otherwise.

"Great. So we're on the same page, then," Trevor says.

I lean my hip against the counter and slowly sweep my gaze across the room. It's late afternoon, so it's starting to get quieter. This is the time Branum normally comes in.

And yep, there he is, sitting in what's become his usual spot, a small table with a direct line of sight to the front counter. He's wearing a red-and-black flannel shirt over a white tee. His messenger bag is flung open on the table, books and papers scattered about in front of him. I wonder what he's studying.

And yep, like always, he's looking this way.

This way, not *at me*.

Important distinction.

"Same page?" I turn back to my boss. "What are you talking about?"

Trevor turns so his back is to Branum and lifts a hand. "You're a cute guy." He lifts his other hand. "He's a fucking mountain god sent from the heavens above." He smooshes his palms together and rubs them like they're sticks and he's trying to start a fire.

I tap each of my fingers against my thumb three times before coming out with, "Anyone ever tell you your worldview of the complexities of gay relationships is highly nuanced?"

Trevor smiles. "Anyone ever tell you that you're not as good at deflecting and playing dumb as you think you are? Come on. Tell me the truth. You know he's here for you, right?"

"He's here to read. Or study, by the looks of things."

"He's here to check out the stunningly cute, new-in-town librarian. Trust me. I know."

"How?"

"PJ, darling. I've worn my tightest, most butt-hugging pants all week. I've sauntered and shimmied around that man every time he comes in. And has he dragged his eyes away from you to me even once during that time? N. O. Fuck the books, and fuck reading. It's you. That man is here for *you*."

Well, when he puts it like that.

"I have books to shelve," I tell him. "And for the record, you have a great ass, and I'm sure someone, someday soon, will appreciate it."

Trevor makes the fingers crossed gesture, and I set off on my way. My trolley is perfectly organized as always, enabling me to start at the far end of the general fiction section and move through the books row by row until I reach history.

I'm easing the trolley around a corner into the next aisle when two teenagers break apart and scurry away. I chuckle to myself. Is it wrong that it warms my heart a little that teenagers are still making out in libraries?

Can't say I ever had that experience growing up. Hard to find time to make out with someone when you're dodging bullies and getting picked on mercilessly every day. High school was a nightmare. My sexuality and my mental health issues collided, and it wasn't fun. I was literally counting down the days until it was over and I could get the hell out of there.

Most kids leave small towns for the big city.

Not me.

I knew the noise, the rush of traffic, the crowds of people would be too much chaos for me to handle.

I lived in a couple of other small towns, but it never really worked. But from the moment the Greyhound dropped me off on the main street in Thickehead, it felt right. There's something magical about this place and the people who live here. They celebrate diversity and difference. Maybe that's why I gelled with it so quickly.

I'm returning books, lost in my thoughts, and I'm not really paying attention, so as I turn, I run smack bang into someone.

A very tall, very solid someone.

A strong, calloused hand grips my right bicep, preventing me from toppling over.

"Sorry. Didn't mean to startle you."

"It's fine. You didn't." I straighten and pat down the front of my shirt. Branum pulls his hand away.

"Can I help you with anything?" I ask, gazing into his browny-gray eyes.

"I'm good. Was just getting a book."

He lifts the book he's holding, but I don't pay any attention to it.

I can't.

First he did something, and now I've done something, and that's the only thing I can think about. My brain, when it latches on to something like this, is like a dog with a bone.

Branum touched my right bicep. I brushed my left hand down my shirt four times. The fingertips on my right hand twitch, and my mind goes into overdrive, needing the movements to be repeated on the opposite sides for symmetry.

Need to find balance. If I don't, the scales tip and all hell will break loose.

Yeah, this is my brain talking. It really is no fun being me sometimes.

"You okay, PJ?"

I drop my gaze and stare at the carpet. Shame and embarrassment flood me. It's like being back in high school all over again. I hated getting bullied, but what I hated more was that I kinda agreed with the bullies. I was a freak, a weirdo, and every other name they taunted me with.

And I still am.

My chin starts to quiver but stops when it's greeted by Branum's fingers. With a gentle strength, he lifts my chin until our eyes meet.

This is...good.

Great, actually.

My chin is central so he's not technically touching my left or right side, potentially throwing me even more off-balance than I already am.

"What do you need?"

Even as he whispers, his voice remains powerful. Commanding. Safe.

A tear skates down my cheek. "You'll think it's stupid."

"I won't," he growls lowly. "I promise."

I break free from his hold and look away. "Can you...touch my left arm please? Like you did my right arm before."

Without hesitating or questioning my ridiculous request, he presses my left bicep with the same amount of strength he used on my right. With him holding me, I swipe my right hand down the front of my shirt exactly four times.

"Thank you," I whisper once I'm done.

Then I retreat.

With trembling hands, I steer the trolley away from there, away from the man I just humiliated myself in front of.

After that mortifying little display, I'd be willing to bet that's the last time I ever see Branum Grady Duncan.

5

Branum

I lean against the handrail when I reach the top step. A couple of school kids pass me, hushing their talk as the automatic doors slide open and they step into the library. I glance inside after them, hoping to get a glimpse of PJ, but I don't see him.

What the fuck happened yesterday?

I still don't know myself.

I've been replaying the interaction over in my mind, but I'm just as confused as ever. Why did PJ ask me to hold his other arm while he brushed his shirt? What was that about?

The only answer I can come up with is that maybe it was some sort of ritual, but yeah, that's pretty weak and doesn't make a whole lot of sense. But it's all that I've got.

I tug on the strap of my messenger bag and head inside, determined to get some answers out of PJ. And I don't just mean about what happened yesterday. I've never raised seeing him on my property last week, and neither has he.

That changes today.

The air-con blows down on me as I enter through the sliding doors, making the ends of my long hair move. I've gotten used to that, as well as to the specific library smell. I never would've guessed that books emitted a scent, but they do. It was a bit strange at first, but it's grown on me.

I park myself in my usual spot, on the lookout for PJ as I set out my folders and notes on the table. He's usually either behind the counter or meandering through the rows of books. A couple of times, he's been out the back and I haven't seen him right away. Looks like today is going to be one of those days.

I open my black folder and glance down at the notebook I keep hidden inside it. There's no way I want people to see what I'm actually studying.

Literacy Works: Learning to Read for Adults.

Harrick helped me order these books online. Apparently they

have great reviews and are effective at teaching semiliterate adults like me how to read in as little as fourteen weeks. There's really no need for me to come to the library since I could read them at home...but then I'd miss out on seeing PJ.

It's funny in a way. Our little *exchange* yesterday only makes me even more curious about him than I already was.

He strikes me as being a bit unusual, but in an intriguing way. In a way that makes me want to learn more about him.

Not that I'm deluding myself by thinking he'd be interested in a simple guy like me. I work hard, I like the outdoors, and I eat a lot. That's about all there is to me. Why would a smart and interesting guy like PJ give me the time of day?

I've never been able to hold down a long-term relationship. My former partners, all three of them, wanted something I couldn't give. They wanted excitement. They wanted adventure. They wanted big-city life.

I'm a mountain man, through and through. I spent my whole childhood on the move, from big cities to small towns in the middle of nowhere to everywhere in between. I'm thirty-two and know what I want, and what I want is a quiet, settled life in Thickehead.

I like the people here, the way of life, the beauty of the place, and most of all, the stability.

Plus, it's nice being close to my brothers. Family is the most important thing to me. We survived a crazy childhood, and nothing makes me happier than living so close to Harrick and Marsh, being in each other's lives, and knowing that we're only a phone call and a short drive away from each other should anything happen.

I don't know what brought PJ here or how long he intends on staying, but I know I can't leave.

I check the time. I've been here for almost half an hour, and there's still no sign of him. I get up and walk over to the front counter.

"Hello?"

The man spins around. I've seen him here every day, too. Think he might be the boss librarian dude. His name badge tells me his name is Tr...ev...or.

He smiles widely. "Can I take a guess?"

"Excuse me?"

"A guess. If I guess correctly what question you're about to ask me, I win."

What is it about library staff? Are they all this wacky?

"*Okay*. Go on then."

"Good. In that case, I'd be willing to bet a date that—"

"Wait. What? No." I raise my hand to stop him. "I don't... I mean... No offense, but I don't want to take you out on a—"

"Let me finish, then you can resume your sputtering."

I lift a brow. Sassy dude, this one.

"I'd be willing to bet a date...as in, *you* ask *PJ* out on a date, not me...that the question you came over here to ask is, where is PJ today?" He rocks on his feet, smiling brightly. "Am I right?"

Well, color me pink. "You are." I scowl. "How did you know?"

Trevor rolls his eyes. "You're just as clueless as he is."

"Clueless?"

"PJ had some errands to run so I gave him the day off."

"I see. Great. Well, thanks, Trevor."

I turn to leave, and he clears his throat.

"Yes?"

His smile widens. "Our bet?"

"I thought you were kidding."

He shakes his head, still grinning. "I wasn't. Next time you see PJ, you're asking him out on a date. Deal?"

He stretches his hand out. I stare at him for a few seconds before shaking it. "Yeah, okay. Deal."

I don't know what the exact ordering system in the library is, but my favorite books in the world are the ones that need to be stacked on the lower shelves, because as I turn the corner PJ disappeared around a moment ago, I'm greeted by the splendid sight of him bent over, arranging books on the bottom shelf.

His pert ass is delectable. Everything about him is. His tiny frame. His wild red mane. His mismatched eyes.

And if you want to do more than just ogle the guy like some pathetic loser, you're going to have to keep to your end of the bargain you made yesterday, and ask the guy out.

Easier said than done.

The library is about to close, and in the two hours I've been here—staring at PJ and not studying like I should be—I haven't worked up the courage to ask him out on a date.

I clear my throat so I don't startle him. PJ straightens and spins around to face me. "Oh, hi, Branum."

His voice is a little shaky, and I can't help but wonder if I intimidate him. I'd hate it if I did. I may be bigger and stronger than him, but I never want him to be afraid of me.

My shoulders tense as I start to speak. "I... There's... I'd like to ask you something."

PJ places the three books he's holding on the trolley, then taps it twice with his index and middle finger. "Is it about the weird thing I made you do the other day?"

I shake my head. "No. That wasn't it."

He lets out a sigh. "Shit. Is it about me seeing you at the river?"

I shake my head again and smile. "Nope. Not that either."

"Maybe I should just shut up and let you talk? Sorry. Go ahead."

This is it. The moment of truth. Adrenaline spikes in my veins. I open my mouth. "PJ, would you like to have dinner with me?"

6

PJ

Is Branum asking me out on a date? Is that what's happening right now?

Howww?

Whyyy?

When he approached, I'd expected him to drill me about my weird behavior the other day...not ask me out to dinner.

"Um, are you sure?"

Fuck, shit, fuck, shit. That's literally the worst thing I could have said.

"Of course I'm sure."

He looks at me with those dark-brown eyes and a soft smile on his lips, and something inside of me melts. He really is asking me out.

"Um, okay. Yes. I would... I'd like that. Thank you."

Correction. *That's* the worst thing I could have said. Who the fuck thanks someone for asking them out? PJ Henderson, that's who.

"What sort of food do you like?" he asks, ignoring my stupidity, thank god.

"You might not be able to tell by looking at me, but I love all the food, and I want to eat as much of it as possible."

That makes him smile. "Can I confess something?"

"Sure."

"I was going to suggest that new French restaurant that's just opened up because I wanted you to think that I was fancy and sophisticated, but..."

"But what?"

His smile grows. "The Pancake Pantry has an all-you-can-eat buffet every Wednesday night."

A small giggle escapes me. For someone so big and scary looking, Branum's actually quite gentle.

"I loooove pancakes."

"Great." He lets out a dazzling smile. "Can I pick you up at seven?"

"Sounds good." I pull out the small notepad I always carry. "Let me give you my address."

~

Why did Wednesday have to be so far away?

Okay, so in reality it's only been slightly longer than forty-eight hours since Branum asked me out, but these past two days have stretched out for an eternity. To make matters worse, Branum hasn't set foot in the library yesterday or today. It's the first time he hasn't come in since I spotted him by the river a few weeks ago.

Has something happened? Is something wrong? I gave him my address, but we didn't exchange numbers, so there's no way for me to find out.

Well, there is one way.

I glance at the time. It's five to seven, and I'm dressed and ready to go.

The question is, will Branum show up?

Trevor sure seemed to think so. He's been buzzing with excitement ever since I told him Branum had asked me out. He seemed almost a little *too* invested, the way he carried on about it.

He didn't think it was a big deal that Branum hadn't shown up these past two days. I wish I shared his confidence.

There's a loud knock on the door. I almost jump out of my skin.

He's here.

Okay, so I can stop panicking about Branum not showing up and start freaking out about the fact that I have a date with a smoking-hot mountain man.

I open the front door, and there he is, wearing a black button-up, dark jeans that cling to his tree-trunk-sized thighs, and slightly scuffed western boots. He's clutching something wrapped in brown paper and smiling...almost a little bashfully.

"Wow, PJ. You look incredible."

Do not question the man. Do not say really.

"Thanks."

Yay me.

He eyes me up and down. I wasn't sure what to wear so I went for my favorite pair of khakis and a simple white button-up. Judging by the smile growing on his lips, I think I made the right decision.

"Here. This is for you."

I take the package from him. "You got me a gift?"

"It's no big deal."

"Can I open it?"

"Of course. Please do."

I unwrap it carefully since I have no idea what it could be and smile when I see the book cover.

Hiking Trails in and around Thickehead.

"This is really thoughtful. Thank you so much."

"It's nothing. Just don't want you trespassing on anyone else's property."

"When was I trespassing?"

"When you saw me by the river you were actually on my land."

I clutch my chest. "Oh my god, I was?"

Branum grins. "You were. And I'm very glad you were, don't get me wrong, but I don't want you getting lost in the forest, that's all."

I start to smile, then get hit by a sensation that throws me off-balance. Mentally, that is. The excitement leading up to this date, Branum actually showing up, the unexpected kindness of his gift, the fact I was trespassing on his land without realizing it... It all grows in my head and becomes too much.

"You okay, PJ?"

"Yeah. I'm fine."

Branum takes a step closer and lowers his gaze. "Are you sure?"

I nod. I don't want to tell him what's going on with me, hoping that it'll pass quickly, so I stick with something safe. "I didn't realize I was on your property. Guess I'm in shock. I'm so sorry."

"No need to apologize. If you hadn't accidentally come onto my land, who knows if we'd have met."

"That's...true."

Then my mind revisits Branum stripping, diving into the water, floating on his back, touching himself...

And yep, I'm officially dizzy.

I waver on my feet, but before I have the chance to completely humiliate myself by doing something like keeling over, Branum's hands are on me and he's leading me inside the house, guiding me toward the couch.

"Can I get you some water or anything else?"

"No. No. I'm okay... Thank you."

He studies me for a moment. "Change of plans," he announces.

"You're ending the date?" I say meekly, only half kidding.

"Not on your life." He pulls out his cell phone. "But I am bringing the pancakes to us."

Half an hour later, my tiny dining table is covered by what I'm pretty sure is every variety of pancake the Pancake Pantry sells.

I've fully recovered, thankfully.

I don't know why I got faint, but after excusing myself to splash some water on my face and do some circular breathing to calm down, I feel a lot better.

So despite the less-than-stellar start—which was entirely my fault—the date is actually going pretty well.

I think.

So, uh, this could be my first date.

Okay, it totally *is* my first date, so all I'm going by is the fact that Branum is still here. He could've split after I nearly blacked out, but instead he ordered a truckload of food, and now we're sitting here, eating and talking.

That counts as a good date, right?

"What made you come to Thickehead?" Branum asks, opening another container of pancakes. The man has an appetite.

"I like small towns," I tell him. "I got the job in the library before I arrived, so I thought I'd give it six months to see if I like it."

"How long have you been here?"

"Almost two months."

"And your verdict? Do you like it?... Are you going to stay?"

Heat swirls in his eyes, and I like it... It almost feels like he wants me to stay. Unless I'm imagining it because that's what I'd *like* to believe.

"I think I will," I answer, cutting into my blueberry pancake. "It's not a bad place, despite the badly signed hiking trails that lead unsuspecting people onto private property."

Branum smiles as he chews. "I'll let the ranger know."

"What about you? Have you always lived here?"

"No. My dad and my brothers, we moved around a lot. This was one of many places we briefly passed through. But I liked it so much I came back."

"You own the timber yard, don't you?"

He chuckles. "God, this really is a small town. I do." Then he directs his gleaming eyes at me. "And you're into birdwatching?"

I almost choke on my pancake. "How do you know that?"

"Small town. You remember a guy called Eddie?"

"Of course. I ran into him when I got here. Nice guy."

"He is. He's also dating my brother. When I told them I'd be spending more time at the library, Eddie mentioned he suggested the hiking trail near my place to you."

"Ah, got it."

We eat in silence for a while.

Some people might not like this aspect of small-town living, everyone being in everyone else's business. It doesn't bother me. In fact, I like it. It makes me feel like I belong to something.

"So." I wipe at the corners of my mouth. "What brings you to the library every day? It looks like you're studying something."

7

Branum

I stop, mid-chew.

It's the one question I'd been hoping to avoid, but of course he'd ask. How is PJ to know the real, pathetic reason behind my visits to the library?

It's one thing to tell Harrick and Eddie. They reacted well, and when I caught up with my older brother, Marsh, a few days ago, he was supportive, too.

But PJ is someone new.

Someone I like.

Someone I hope might like me.

And not graduating from high school and barely being able to read isn't going to make a great impression. He's a librarian for Pete's sake. It's a safe bet to assume he loves books and literature. This could be as much of a deal breaker for him as someone who wants to live in the city is for me.

Fuck.

But I have to tell him the truth. I don't want there to be any lies or miscommunications between us. Ever.

Even if it means there may not be an *us* after he finds out.

I lower my knife and fork and tell him everything, from dropping out of school when I was fourteen, to not being able to read very well, and about my goal to change that and get my GED.

"Wow." He leans back in his chair when I'm done. "That's... amazing. I'm really happy for you."

"You are?"

"Of course." He nods, causing a lock of hair to fall across his forehead. "What you're doing is so great. You should be proud of yourself."

He...he doesn't think I'm an idiot.

"Thank you for saying that."

He reaches over and strokes my hand, making small circles

with his long, delicate fingers. "You can always rely on a ginger not to be judgmental."

He's smiling, but I pick up on an undercurrent of something more serious beneath his words.

"Thank you."

"You have nothing to thank me for." He traces a circle across the top of my other hand. "If there's anything I can do to help in any way, please let me know."

"You can help me get through these." I look over the massive spread on the table.

PJ throws his head back and laughs. "I can definitely do that."

After demolishing dinner—PJ was right, he could eat a lot. Not as much as me but an impressive amount for a guy his size, nonetheless—we retired to his living room.

His house is small and a little bare, but I suppose that makes sense since he's only been here a little while. The one part that's packed, though? That'd be the bookcases—yes, plural—that take up two entire living room walls.

When he excused himself to go to the bathroom, I took a closer look, pulling a few of the books out. They all seem to be romance novels. Seems like PJ here is a bit of a romantic.

"Have you seen any cool birds since you got here?" I ask him.

"All birds are cool," he points out with a twinkle in his eye before rattling off a list of the ones he's spotted.

"That's impressive."

"I'm really hoping to see a mountain bluebird, but they're pretty rare."

"Well, you're welcome to trespass on my land anytime you like. I have some good vantage points I could take you to."

"Really?"

I nod.

He ponders it for a few moments, and I wonder what—or *who*

—in his life has made him so cautious. Finally, his face lights up. "That'd be awesome."

"My pleasure."

We're sitting next to each other on the couch, but he's too far away for me to do the old *yawn and reach my arm around him* move.

But I want to touch him. I want to touch him so freaking much.

PJ is captivating. He's interesting. He's so fucking cute.

He's unlike anyone I've ever met.

And he knows about my inability to read and that I didn't finish high school, and he didn't balk. His reaction was actually pretty damn sweet.

"Since you've told me something about yourself," he begins demurely. "There's something you should probably know about me."

"What is it?"

He dips his head as he begins talking. "I have OCD." He's speaking softly, so I lean in to make sure I hear him properly. "It stands for obsessive compulsive disorder. It means I sometimes... do...things that might seem a little strange."

He glances up at me, and I register what he's referring to. That time in the library when he asked me to grab his other arm while he patted down the front of his shirt.

"Go on. I'd like to know more."

"I got the official diagnosis when I was fourteen. Most of the time, it's manageable, but then other times, like at the library the other day, I become overwhelmed and need to do this...this rebalancing thing."

"Rebalancing?"

"Yeah. It's like I get thrown off-kilter in my head, and I need to touch or tap or do certain things in a certain way, a certain number of times, evenly, to restore the balance. When I do it, it calms me down and resets me. But if for some reason I can't or don't, I'm unable to function until I do."

"I see. I'm sure I don't understand everything, but thank you for explaining it in a way that helps me understand you a bit better."

PJ hesitates, then asks, "You don't think I'm a freak?"

"I just ate over twenty pancakes. If anyone here is a freak, it's me."

That makes him giggle, and the sound pummels straight into my chest. I like making him happy.

We spend the next few hours talking and getting to know each other better. I tell him about some of the more interesting places I lived growing up, while he tells me what PJ stands for. It's Paul Jean. Apparently, his mom was set on the name Jean Paul but his father hated it, so they compromised and settled on Paul Jean, which PJ hated, and that's why he prefers to go by his initials.

At some point, he scoots down the sofa until our legs are touching. I drape my arm around his shoulder, and he doesn't seem to mind.

When I finally notice the time, it's past midnight. I need to be up in less than five hours.

Reluctantly, I tell him I have to go. He walks me to the front door. There's something in the air, floating like fireflies between us.

"I've got a few big days coming up at work, so I won't be able to make it to the library."

"Is that why you haven't been in the last two days?"

I nod. "Yeah. We're swamped at the moment."

"I see. That's fine."

The sadness in his voice hits me hard. "Hey." I take hold of his chin, lifting it so that our eyes meet. "I really enjoyed tonight, and I would love to see you again."

He blinks up at me with those dual-colored eyes. "You would?"

He has no freaking idea how much. "I would. You free this Saturday?"

"I work in the morning, but I finish at midday."

"Great. I can pick you up from the library, and we can go on a hike? See if we can hunt down that elusive mountain bluebird."

"I'd like that."

"I'd like that, too."

I lean down and place a kiss...on his cheek. "Goodnight, PJ."

"Uh, goodnight, Branum."

8

PJ

"He. Did. What?" Trevor whisper-shouts each word.

I stop scanning books and let out a despondent sigh. "He kissed me on the cheek and left."

"And by cheek you mean..."

"The one on my face."

"Right."

We exchange a look. That was *not* how I pictured my date ending last night.

I thought everything had been going well, aside from when I almost passed out at the start. The conversation flowed easily. Branum revealed something real about himself, which gave me the strength and confidence to do the same.

My OCD has been a deal breaker with guys in the past. All of them ran for the hills as soon as they found out, but Branum didn't seem bothered by it, just like I wasn't bothered by his admission. Like I told him, I think it's great he's learning to read and going for his GED.

I tried to be discreet about it, but during the course of the evening, I slowly inched my way down the couch toward Branum. When I got close enough, he put an arm over my shoulder and held me close.

All the signs were there, pointing to an end-of-date kiss. On the mouth.

I got a cheek.

"What the hell does it mean?" I ask Trevor.

"Beats me." He thinks about it. "Are you seeing him again?"

I nod. "This Saturday. We're going for a hike."

"Who suggested it? You or him?"

"He did. I told him I'm dying to see a mountain bluebird, and he mentioned he's got some good viewing spots on his property."

"Hmm." Trevor strokes his chin. "And the kiss on the cheek happened *after* you revealed you're a birdwatcher?"

"Hey." I jab his side. "No making fun of me. You promised."

Trevor snickers. "I did. I'm sorry. I was just messing around. Look, kiddo, I have no idea what's up with the cheek kiss. You'll just have to ask him when you see him next."

I groan. "Do I have to?"

"Yes."

"Why?"

"Because that's what adults in, or about to be in, or wanting to be in, relationships do. They talk. Like, you know, those words you like to read in your smutty romance novels, but in real life and coming out through your lips. And by lips, I mean—"

"I get it. I get it."

With a heavy sigh, I tap each of my fingers against my thumbs five times. "You're right," I grumble, really wishing he wasn't.

But if I said or did something wrong, or if Branum isn't interested in me that way and just wants to be buddies, I should probably find out now before I get too attached to the guy.

9

Branum

"You did *what*?" Marsh asks.

I drop my head into my hands, let out a loud groan, and repeat, "I kissed him on the cheek."

"And by cheek you mean...?"

I give him the middle finger, and my older brother shuts up.

"Well, I hate to be the one to say it, but you fucked up big-time, bro. What the fuck were you thinking?"

"I don't know. I..." I lift my head. "I wanted to be romantic?"

"By kissing the dude on the cheek? Look I'm hardly Mr. Romance myself, but even I know that move needs to stay in the 1940s where it belongs."

"It wasn't a move. I was... Look, PJ reads romance. You should see his bookcases, man. They're filled with them."

Marsh straightens his legs, resting his boots on my coffee table. "Still not following."

"I wanted our first kiss to be...unforgettable."

"Well, you achieved that. I doubt he'll ever forget that moment."

I growl in frustration. "I wanted to give him something special. When he was in the bathroom, I flicked open one of the books. I'm not sure if I read it properly, but the scene was of two guys having their first kiss on a beach, I think. The sun was setting, the water was lapping at their feet. All that sappy, lovey-dovey stuff... I wanted our first kiss to be the same."

"I've got good news and bad news." Marsh drops his feet to the floor.

"Go on," I say warily.

"The good news is I can see where you're coming from, and it's kinda...sweet. In its own weird way."

"And the bad news?"

"You still kissed him on the cheek."

I let out a defeated yelp and drop my head again. "I'm an idiot. I've fucked everything up."

"No. You haven't. By some miracle, he's agreed to see you again."

I look up at my brother. "Yeah. So?"

"So it means you have a chance to make it right. You might have messed up the first kiss, but, by god, Branum, don't fuck up the second. Because then you will really be an idiot."

10

PJ

Branum smells...different.

Nice. But different.

I first caught a whiff of his cologne when he picked me up from the library at the end of my shift, just like we'd arranged.

He hugged me. It was a solid, middle-of-the-road hug. More than just a passing touch, but not reuniting with a relative after a few years apart, either. I was...happy with it.

Hey, it's better than a kiss on the cheek.

But in all the times he's dropped by the library, I haven't known him to wear cologne. It smells expensive. And it's fine. But it doesn't smell like him.

We've been sitting on the edge of a small peak for about twenty minutes. He was right about having some great birdwatching spots on his property. There's enough of a clearing to provide a good view, but the spot is also tucked away, meaning the birds hopefully won't see us and will feel free to, you know, do their bird thing in front of us.

The thing about birdwatching is that, for obvious reasons, it's a quiet endeavor. So we're not speaking. We didn't talk a whole bunch on the way over here either. He just asked me how my day was, and I asked him how his work was going. That was about the extent of it.

I haven't broached the non-kissing elephant in the room.

Neither has he.

We also haven't spotted the mountain bluebird, but to be honest, as much as I normally love birdwatching, I'd prefer to spend our time together talking rather than in silence.

"I say we call it a day," I announce, resting my binoculars in my lap.

"You sure? I've got time. Don't mind me. I love being outdoors."

I brought a spare pair of binoculars for Branum, but after a cursory look, he seems happy sitting next to me and staring out at the view.

I turn to face him. He's wearing a white button-up that shows off his massive round shoulders and bulging arm muscles. He also brought a blanket and a picnic basket.

Suppose it's time to do the adulting thing and get this issue resolved.

"So," we both say at the same time.

I giggle nervously.

"Sorry, you go first," Branum says.

"Um, okay. Thanks..." I inhale sharply. "Why didn't you kiss me?"

Branum winces but doesn't look too caught off guard by my question. Was he expecting it? Has he been thinking about the non-kiss, too?

"Because I'm an idiot," he says softly, picking at a loose thread on the red-and-white blanket. "And because I wanted our first kiss to be special."

"I...don't understand."

He looks at me. "You read a ton of romance, right?"

"Yeah."

"I wanted to give you something like that, something like what you'd read in a romance novel."

My chest comes alive with butterflies, and I swoon. I freaking swoon. "Are you serious?"

He drops his head and nods.

"Branum, that is so sweet."

"I messed it up, though."

"No, you didn't... Okay, actually yes, you did. But it's okay. The idea is amazing."

"The execution, not so much."

"Hey. Stop beating yourself up about it. I thought I'd said or done something wrong, and that's why I asked. If I'd known you wanted to make the moment special, I would have happily waited. Trust me, I've waited my whole life to meet someone who doesn't run away the second they find out about me."

Branum frowns. "What do you mean?"

"Look at me. I'm a nerdy, neurodivergent librarian. My hair is fire-engine red. My eyes aren't the same color. I have these gross freckles all over my face. And I'm so tiny you could probably lift me up with one arm."

The line on Branum's forehead fades. "Why are you listing all the things I like about you?"

I tilt my head. "I can't tell if you're being serious or not."

"I'm *serious.*" He moves closer and wraps his giant paw around my tiny-in-comparison fingers. "PJ. I've never met anyone like you. I love that you're nerdy and neurodivergent. It makes you smart and unique. I keep wanting to reach out and run my fingers through your hair. You have the most beautiful eyes I've ever seen. Your freckles aren't gross, they're fucking adorable. And I'm not mad about you being tiny, either. I like the idea of being able to pick you up."

I blink. "Wow."

Yep, that's all I've got, folks. Hey, at least I'm not going *really?*

"You intrigue me, and the more I discover about you, the more I want to learn. I've been beating myself up about my non-kiss mistake for days. I'm sorry I made you think it was about you. It wasn't. It's me." He plucks at his shirt. "I'm a simple guy. I don't know how to do romance."

"Is that why you're wearing cologne?"

"I bought the most expensive one I could find." He grimaces. "You don't like it?"

"No, no, it's...fine. It's just...not you."

"I was trying to impress you, like a leading man in a romance novel."

This. Guy.

"You don't have to *try* to impress me. Believe me, I'm all aboard the Branum train."

"So I haven't fucked things up?"

"You haven't." I lean over and stroke his thick beard. "Wow. This is so much softer than I thought it would be."

He smiles shyly. "I bought some fancy-ass beard oil, too."

"That can stay."

Our eyes meet, his smile grows.

He opens his mouth. "I really like yo—"

Something flaps right above Branum's head.

"Holy shit!" I pull back and fumble for my binoculars, bringing them to my eyes as fast as I can.

"What is it?"

I don't answer straightaway.

There, soaring in the mid-afternoon sky, is a mountain bluebird. Now, it's not a majestic bird. We're not in bald eagle territory here. Mountain bluebirds are much smaller. They're delicate but scrappy, so I guess I relate.

I'm tracking a bright turquoise-blue bird, which means it's a male as the females are a duller blue with a gray chest.

"It's a mountain bluebird," I mutter after a few moments, then hand Branum my binoculars. "Here. Have a look."

He takes them from me and his head bobs around a bit as he searches for the bird. I can tell the second he spots it because his lips stretch into a wide, toothy smile. "It's beautiful," he murmurs, not taking his eyes off it.

My body fills with heat, my attraction to this man ratcheting up to a whole new stratosphere. He's so much more than just a gorgeous mountain man. He's kind and considerate and romantic, even if he doesn't realize it.

But he will.

The second he lowers those binoculars, I'll show him just how much I really like him, too.

11

Branum

The mountain bluebird isn't big, but it is truly beautiful.

But that's not what's making my heart dance away in my chest. No. That'd be due to us putting the first-kiss debacle behind us. I'm glad PJ gets where I was coming from, even if I did manage to screw it up royally.

He's not mad, which means I'm in with a shot for a kiss do-over, and this time, I'm not going to fuck it up.

I begin to lower the binoculars when two small warm hands wrap around mine. PJ takes the binoculars from me and rests them on the picnic blanket, then those same warm hands are cupping the sides of my face, and an equally warm body is straddling me.

I stare into his incredible dual-colored eyes. I'll never tire of seeing them, they're spellbinding. *He's* spellbinding.

His lips quirk as he gazes deeply at me. "I really like you, and it means a lot to me that you like me..." He closes his eyes. "All of me. Even the parts no one else does."

I curl a finger into a bright lock of red hair. "If that's the case, people are idiots. There is so much to like about you, PJ."

And with him on my lap, the sun beating down on us, and the sounds of bird calls filling the air, I lean down, and our lips meet for the first time.

He tastes so sweet, and instantly, I want more, but I rein my impulses in. Slow and steady. Tender and delicate. That's how PJ deserves to be kissed, and, goddammit, that's what I'm going to give him.

He sinks into my lap, the hardness in his khakis rubbing against the hardness in my too-tight, way-too-expensive jeans I ordered online.

I snake my arm around his waist as I deepen the kiss, setting about mapping the inside of his mouth, committing every part of it to memory.

He lowers his body even more, and as we kiss, he slowly begins rocking his hips against me. I drop both hands to his round ass and grind him down onto me.

PJ's fingers scrape through my beard, sending pleasure coursing through my entire body. He speeds up his hip rolling as his tongue spears into my mouth.

"Want this," he pants. "Want you."

Is he...is he talking about more than just kissing? Does he want to do more?

"What are you saying, baby?" I murmur around our kiss.

He pulls back, holding my face firmly in his hands. "I want you to fuck me."

"Here? Now?"

He grins. "Yes and yes... If you want to."

"Of course I do, it's just..."

"Just what?"

"I need to ask you this. Are you a virgin, PJ?"

A splash of color ignites his cheeks. "I am."

He lowers his head, and I latch on to his chin to raise it, to look him in the eyes. "This is a big deal. Are you sure it's what you want?"

"It is."

I let go of his chin, and he tilts his head. "I feel something for you. Something I've never felt before. And I know it doesn't mean that we're going to be forever necessarily, but it does mean that this feels right. I want my first time to be with you."

"I want to be with you, too," I tell him, not bothering to correct him about the one thing he got wrong.

That same instinct I've honed over the years to help me evade danger is now sending me a new message, clear as fucking day—This *is* forever.

12

PJ

I go back to kissing Branum, rubbing myself against him like an animal in heat.

Who am I right now?

I've never done anything remotely this wild before. Then again, I've never felt so consumed by desire before.

This is what I want. What I *truly* want. And I know that even when the heat of the moment dissipates, I won't ever regret what we're about to do.

Heck, I even came prepared. I wasn't sure how things would go after our first-kiss convo, but I'm sure glad I stopped off at the drugstore yesterday and picked up condoms and a few packets of lube.

Branum's hands have been on my ass for a while, but as the kiss becomes more frenzied, he starts kneading my cheeks with his strong hands, inching toward the middle. My hole twitches in response, ready, eager, *willing* to be opened up for the very first time.

Branum lifts me off him with as much ease as I expected. He doesn't even make a sound or change his expression as he lowers me onto the blanket, making sure my head is supported the whole time. He grabs a small cushion and places it under my head before proceeding to unbutton my floral shirt. Once it's open, heat lights up his dark eyes as he takes me in.

"So fucking beautiful," he growls before descending on my nipple.

"Wow!" Sparks of pleasure fizzle through my body as he laps and nips at one nub, before moving over to the next.

Ah, the perfect balance.

Branum keeps all his movements symmetrical. If he grazes my left arm, he'll do the same to my right. When he brushes his fingers down the left side of my abs, he repeats the movement down the right.

He peers up at me. "Am I doing this okay?"

I could burst with happiness. "Perfect."

He doesn't need to be doing this, and it's not even something I need right now, but the fact that he's going to this effort for me... It only confirms what I knew even more—This is right.

Branum reaches my belt buckle, unclasps it, then threads it through the belt loops and casts it aside.

His thumbs rest on the waistband of my pants, and he looks up with a mischievous grin. "Got a question I've been meaning to ask you."

"Yeah?"

His grin becomes a smile. "Yeah. Does the carpet match the drapes?"

I laugh. "Only one way to find out."

He pulls down my pants and underwear with one rough yank, his eyes bulging as he notices my neatly trimmed bush and gets the answer to his question. He skims his fingertips through my bright ginger pubes.

"How do you keep getting better and better?" he murmurs.

I'm hoping it's a rhetorical question, because I wouldn't know how to answer if it isn't.

I feel the same way about him. The more I get to know Branum, the stronger my feelings for him become.

He takes my erect cock in his hands, and a shiver runs through me. No one's ever touched me there. As he slowly starts to jerk me off, I close my eyes and lose myself in the pleasure running through my entire body.

A few moments later, something warm and wet engulfs me. My eyes burst open, then go impossibly wide at the sight of Branum, the big burly mountain man, bobbing up and down on my cock.

He glances up at me and, with his mouth full of my cock, winks.

A very unsexy giggle escapes me, but before I have a chance

to get embarrassed, Branum throats me so deep my entire length disappears inside him.

I fall back onto the blanket and hook my legs around him as he continues bringing me so much pleasure with his mouth.

"So, so goooood," I moan, my fingers charging into his thick hair.

I thought I was destined to be a virgin for a long time. I never expected to find anyone, much less someone who sees me, flaws and all, and doesn't just tolerate or accept me. Branum genuinely likes every part of me. He thinks I'm hot and sexy. He wants me, maybe as much as I want him.

And I really, *really* want him.

"M-m-my turn," I stammer, nudging my fingers into his shoulder.

Branum takes one last lick, like he's trying to suck all the flavor out of a lollipop, before pulling off me.

He licks his lips, smirking. "Fuck, you're delicious."

I don't know how to respond to that, so I just point to the bulge in his ridiculously tight pants. "My turn," I say again.

Branum nods, still smirking, as he undresses.

Now, I have seen him naked before, but the close-up strip show I'm getting now is something else. He loses the white button-up first. My hands instinctively reach out, and I rub up and down his chest, his meaty pecs, and his stomach. He's fit as fuck, that much is clear. I run my hands over his stomach, loving how soft his skin is.

He shuffles back, undoes his jeans, and when he tugs them and his briefs down his legs, the biggest fucking cock springs out. It's long, veiny, and about as thick as my wrist.

"Fuck!" I exclaim. "It's so..."

"We don't have to do anything you're not ready for, baby."

I hear Branum's words. I do. But I'm going to get that monster inside of me...or die trying.

He lowers himself until our faces are at the same level. He

gives me a soft kiss—on the mouth, thankfully—and it's beautiful and sweet and tender.

But right now, I don't want beautiful and sweet and tender.

"I'm ready," I tell him.

He pulls back and stares me deep in the eyes.

"I'm ready for you to fuck me, Branum."

13

Branum

My heart beats heavy in my chest as I absorb the magnitude of what's about to take place.

I've had sex before, but something tells me this time is going to be unlike any other time.

Because of who it's with.

I'm staring into PJ's beautiful mixed-colored eyes, so wrapped up in him, savoring the taste of his cock and his mouth on my tongue, when I suddenly realize something. "Shit."

"What is it?"

"We don't have supplies."

He smirks, reaching over for his khakis and producing something from the back pocket. "Yes." He hands me a condom and three small square packets of lube. "We do."

I let out a relieved laugh. "I could freaking kiss you."

"You'll be doing more than that, mister." PJ laughs, too, then looks around. "Wait. This is totally private property, right? No one can...see us?"

"We're one hundred percent secure here," I tell him. "The only people who ever trespass are super cute, super nerdy, and super neurodivergent librarians, and by my count, Thickehead only has one of those."

He laughs again, and the sound infiltrates my body all the way to my bones. I love making him happy. I love making him moan and feel good. And I have a feeling I'm going to love fucking the life out of him.

PJ lies back down, and I scooch down so I'm closer to his ass. His eyes drift down to my cock.

He gulps. "You have a really big dick."

"I'll be gentle, baby. I promise. We can stop at any time."

He nods and shoots me a look that conveys that he trusts me...or at least that's what I'm reading it as.

"First, I'm going to prep you using my fingers," I say as I begin running some quick math in my head. I've got three packets of lube. Ideally, I'd like three tubs of the stuff, but beggars can't be choosers. I can't even dash back to my cabin, because yeah, it's been that long, and I don't have any supplies. At least one of us was smart enough to think ahead.

"Once you're ready, we'll move on to the next part."

"You mean your cock?"

I smile. "Yes, my cock. Now, before we get started, do you *need* anything?"

He shakes his head, never taking his eyes off me. "No. I feel perfectly...*balanced*."

I smile. I'd been trying to make sure I was as even as possible in all of my movements. "Good. But if that changes, you just let me know, okay?"

"I will."

I tear open the first packet of lube and work a finger in... Then a second... Finally a third.

"Ahhhh..." He sighs, breathing in slowly and evenly as I stretch him out.

"You're doing so well, baby."

"I think I'm ready."

I give a nod. "Yeah. I think you are, too."

I used two packets of lube, leaving just the one for this part, but I thought it was important to get him as prepared as I could.

I'm about to sheathe up when PJ grabs my hand. "Wait. When's the last time you had sex?"

"Uhhh... A *long* time ago."

"Did you get tested after?"

"I did. Negative."

He takes a deep breath, his eyes landing on mine. "Then I'd like for you to fuck me bare. Please."

The way his voice cracks on *please* does me in. I don't need to ask him if he's sure, if this is really what he wants, *how* he wants it, because it's written all over his face.

"What a gift you're giving me," I murmur, brushing my hand down the side of his face.

"I trust you, Branum. I really do."

His words hit me right in the chest, and in that moment, I silently make a vow to always be worthy of this beautiful man's trust. "Thank you."

I toss the condom aside, rip open the last packet of lube, and smear it all over my hard-on.

With PJ on his back, I get into position over him, notching the head of my cock against his ass. He wraps his legs around my lower back, pressing me into him.

"Let me know if you need me to stop."

He curls his hands around the back of my neck, exhaling with a smile. "I will. But I'm ready. I want this... I want *you*."

I reach down and grip my cock as I begin to enter him. PJ keeps his eyes on me the whole time.

"You're doing great," I whisper, sliding deeper into him. Good thing I spent all that time warming him up, because his channel is tight as fuck. Don't get me wrong, it feels incredible, but my number one concern is making sure he's okay.

"All good?" I check.

"Yep," he says on a shaky exhale.

I continue sinking deeper into his body.

PJ's legs lower from my waist. He hooks his heels into my ass and thrusts down, forcing me into him.

"Fuck!" He cries out.

I immediately pull back, but his feet dig into my ass, preventing me from going far.

"You can't break me, Branum. I'm stronger than I look."

I grin. "I have no doubt about that. I just don't want to cause you any—"

"It's going to hurt. It's my first time. But I'm ready. And I want it. *Now*."

Clenching my jaw, I give my PJ what he wants, thrusting into him until my balls slap against his ass. He lets out an almighty roar, his body convulsing as he adjusts to the intrusion.

I pull back slightly and look down.

I've done it.

I've taken him.

He's mine...

PJ locks eyes with me and grins wickedly. "We did it."

"We did."

"Now that the hard part is over, fuck me, Branum. Fuck me with everything you've got."

I don't hold back anymore, letting my primal instincts take over. Our bodies slap together as I lower myself, our mouths kissing messily, and pleasure surges through my body.

I fuck PJ hard.

Rough.

Deep.

I grab his cock and start fisting it.

"Oh, fuck, I'm so close."

"Come," I murmur. "Come for me."

I want to see my sexy, nerdy librarian lose his shit.

"Okay. I'm getting close. Ohhh, fuck. Ohhh, here I —Fuuuuuck!"

PJ's face twists and contorts as his release spurts out of his cock. His whole body spasms as I draw rope after rope of sticky goodness from him.

I've stopped moving, aware that being inside him after he's come might heighten all his senses. It could even be painful.

Carefully, I pull out. He lets out a little whimper and shakes his head, almost as if he's snapping himself out of a dream.

He flips around so his mouth is in front of my cock. He glances up at me, and maybe he's in some post-O delirium, but I swear I've never seen a more ravenous look on a person's face.

"Your turn," he says, his voice heavy with need.

He starts jerking me off with one hand while plopping his

mouth over my swollen head. I'm so close to the edge, there's no way I'm going to last long.

"I'm close," I warn him.

He pulls himself off me. "Good. I want to taste you."

"Okay," I pant, trying to steady myself, but how can I? I've got a gorgeous ginger hungry for my load. Dreams really do come true.

PJ jerks me off with both hands, going faster and faster until my balls lift, and I unleash into his open mouth. Some of the cum misses his mouth and lands on his cheeks, and I swear the contrast of the white release splashing over his red freckles makes me come even more.

When I'm finally done, I reach around for my shirt to wipe PJ's face clean.

The whole time, he's staring into my eyes. I see the trust. The kindness. The intelligence. The quirkiness.

I see all of him, and I want every single bit of it.

One word keeps running through my head.

One word that tells me today marks the first day of a brand-new chapter.

One word that symbolizes everything I feel about PJ.

Forever.

14

PJ

"Did he kiss you? Please tell me he kissed you otherwise I *will* die."

I chuckle quietly at Trevor's dramatics.

"Don't you have a reading hour to get to?"

"Eh. Mrs. Taylor brought in cupcakes. Figure that buys me five minutes. Now..." He strokes his chin. "The fact you're deflecting worries me and makes me think the date didn't go so well. But on the other hand, your skin is positively radiant. So, you either had a *tremendous* date, or I'm going to need the name of the therapist who gave you that kick-ass facial at the Thickehead Day Spa. Which is it, kiddo?"

I grin, not saying a word. I got a kick-ass facial all right, just not at a day spa.

My expression must give me away because Trevor gets up nice and close and whispers, "It's option A. Great date, fabulous sex?"

"No," I whisper back, leaning in. "Great date, *out of this world* sex."

Trevor does an excited golf clap in front of his chest. "Yayyyy. I'm so happy for you."

My grin blooms into a full-on smile. "Yeah, I'm pretty happy for me, too."

And it's not because of the sex. Well, it's not *entirely* because of the sex.

It's finding someone who sees me—sees all of me—and likes me anyway. My nerdiness, my neurosis, my freaking birdwatching. Do you have any idea how many times I've been teased about that in my life?

And the thing with Branum is that he doesn't just put up with it. He isn't being polite or putting on an act. I genuinely believed him when he said he would have happily sat on the ledge beside me in silence for as long as I needed. I can't describe how good that felt and how much that simple gesture meant to me.

That's why him fucking me and fucking me bare was a no-brainer. I don't know what the future holds, but I'd never been more certain of anything than I was in that moment that I wanted to feel him inside me with nothing between us.

"And to think, if Branum hadn't lost the bet, none of this might've happened."

Trevor's words hurtle into my chest, slamming me back to reality.

"Look, I do need to get going. I can see the kids starting to get restless. If you can keep going with these returns that'd be great, and when I get back, I'll grab a few wedding magazines, and we can start making plans."

He's about to skip off when I grab him by the hem of his cardigan.

"What. Did. You. Say?"

He spins around. "Relax. I was just kidding about the magazines—"

"No. Before that." I glare at him. "What. Bet?"

"Oh. Shit." His face falls. "Sorry. I misspoke."

"Well, why don't you *un*-misspeak and tell me what you were referring to?"

"Can I tell you after reading hour? The kids are starting to—"

"The kids will be fine for sixty seconds, which is exactly how long it'll take for you to tell me the freaking truth."

"Fine. But I don't want you getting upset, okay? This is one of those things that sounds worse than it actually is."

"I'll be the judge of that."

"Okay, so remember when I told you about how Branum asked about you on your day off?"

"I do."

"Well, it was a slow day, and I was bored without you, so when Branum came over to the counter, I jokingly said that I knew what question he wanted to ask before he said a word. I then *—very stupidly and without thinking it through or meaning anything* *bad by it*—bet him that if I guessed his question correctly, he would ask you out on a date."

I take a step away from Trevor. "So, the only reason Branum asked me out is because you...bet on it?"

"No no nooooo... See, this is what I meant when I said it sounds worse than it is. Come on, PJ, don't be mad. I can guarantee he would have asked you out anyway."

"Maybe you should stop making bets and guarantees, Trevor. How's that working out for you?" I peer into the reading room. Some of the kids are climbing the wall. Literally. "You should probably go."

Trevor reaches for my arm, but I pull away.

He sighs. "Fine. I'll go. But we'll talk about this later. Please don't misconstrue this. You hate miscommunication in your romance novels, right? Don't be *that guy*."

I'm trying really fucking hard not to be *that guy*, but despite Trevor rushing over to me after children's reading hour and doing his best to placate me, I'm feeling a lot of things in the back seat of the Uber headed for Branum's timber yard.

I bump the side of the door with my right elbow, so I twist around to do the same with my left, keeping an eye on the driver to make sure he doesn't notice in the rearview mirror. Last thing I need right now is to be judged for my OCD.

I manage to successfully make contact, but as I swing back around, my left hand drops to the seat. I tap the seat four times with my left hand, before counting out four taps with my right.

Just breathe, PJ. Try to calm down.

I'm so confused.

On the one hand, I want to trust Branum.

He's been honest with me, even when he didn't need to be. He's never given me any reason to doubt him or suspect his motives.

But the thing I can't get over, the one niggling, annoying thought that keeps rattling around in my head is: did he really only ask me out because he lost a bet?

That's so humiliating.

That hurts.

And it makes me feel like absolute shit because for the first time in my life, I thought I'd finally met a guy who, for real, liked me for me.

And I liked *that* feeling. I liked being open and myself and not hiding any part of me. I've only just had a taste of it, and what, now it's going to get ripped away?

I know I should give Branum the benefit of the doubt, and I want to. We resolved the silly first-kiss issue by talking. Maybe we can do the same with this?

Like Trevor said, it could be one of those situations that sounds worse than it actually is. And I *don't* want to make a scene or do the typical over-the-top thing I hate reading about in my novels, but the pain flooding me is real, and it makes it hard to think straight, to know what's real and what isn't.

The car pulls up at the timber yard, and I mutter a quick thanks to the driver. I head straight for the small admin building and step inside.

"Good afternoon." A friendly-looking, middle-aged lady smiles at me from behind her desk.

"Hi."

"Can I help you, sweetie?"

"Um, yeah." I point to the closed door off to the side that I'm assuming is Branum's office. "Is Branum here?"

"He sure is." She gets up. "Can I tell him—?"

The door swings open, and Branum strides out. He looks sexy as fuck in his navy blue coveralls. He's got the sleeves rolled up, his veiny forearms on display, but I am not focusing on that right now.

"Hey, PJ." He smiles warmly. "What brings you by?"

I drop my head.

Fuck. What was I thinking, coming over here unannounced? I'm an idiot.

"Come inside." Branum gestures to his office, his voice serious. "Hold my calls please, Dee."

"Of course."

With my cheeks on fire, I keep my gaze focused on the wooden floor as I schlep my ass into his office.

With the door closed, Branum approaches...then stops, keeping a few feet between us. "What's wrong?"

I let out a trembling breath, my eyes starting to sting. *Oh god. No, please don't cry.* The only thing worse than being the guy who barges into someone's workplace being all melodramatic and crazy is being the guy who barges into someone's workplace and starts bawling their eyes out.

"Can I get you some water?... Or scotch? Would you like to sit down?"

Branum's deep voice pacifies me a little, and I take a few deep breaths, still avoiding looking at him directly.

Eventually, I lift my head. He looks concerned.

I take another deep breath, look straight into his dark eyes, and ask the question I want to, don't want to, want to, don't want to, but know I have to ask.

"Is the reason you asked me out because you lost a bet with Trevor?"

15

Branum

"Absolutely not," I reply, my hackles rising. "What makes you say that?"

"Trevor. He told me about your bet."

Fuck. So that's why PJ's here. Any hopes I had that he was paying me a friendly visit died the second I laid eyes on him at reception. I knew something was up, but I wasn't expecting him to come out with *this*.

"It wasn't a bet," I counter, trying to keep my voice steady while silently plotting Trevor's demise. What the fuck has that guy told him? And why? Is he trying to come between us?

"So, what was it then?"

"Let's have a seat." I gesture to the sofa by the window.

PJ gives a tentative nod, walks over, and sits down.

"Can I get you some—?"

"No." The word comes out so harshly it seems to take even him by surprise. "Sorry. I just... I just want to know what happened. Please tell me. I'm completely freaking out over here."

I settle on the other side of the couch, giving PJ the space I suspect he needs at the moment.

He looks over at me, his eyes watery, and it makes my stomach clench. I hate seeing him like this. I hate that I'm responsible for him feeling this way.

I need to fix this, and stat. He wants answers, so that's what I'll give him.

"I came in one day, and you weren't there. I went over to the counter and was about to ask about you when Trevor said something like, 'Let me guess what you're going to ask.' I said, 'Fine, go ahead.' That's when he came up with the bet idea. I actually interrupted him because I thought he was implying he wanted to go out with me."

"Why did you stop him?"

"Because he wasn't the librarian I had my eye on. He wasn't

the reason why I came to the library every day when I could have just as easily studied at home."

"Really?"

"Really. I've been infatuated with you since the second I caught a glimpse of you running away in the forest. I'm sorry that me asking you out got caught up in a dumb conversation between Trevor and me, and I'm even more sorry that I didn't have the balls to ask you out the very first time I came to the library."

"Why didn't you?"

"You really want to know?"

He nods, a lock of red hair falling across his forehead.

"Because I thought to myself, why would a smart, beautiful, intriguing guy like you be interested in a dumb lunkhead like me who can't even read properly?"

"Branum!" PJ lifts his hand. "If you ever call yourself dumb again, so help me god, I'll... I'll..." He looks around, like he's trying to find the right word. "I'll hit you."

"You will?"

"Gah, no. Hit is the wrong word. I'm not a violent pers—"

I quirk a brow. "Can I choose where?"

"Where what?"

"Where you hit me."

PJ chews on his lip, looking like he's trying not to smile. "This isn't funny."

"You're right. It's not. I apologize for being a coward and not asking you out earlier, and I'm truly sorry for not being upfront about my conversation with Trevor. I didn't tell you because I was planning on asking you out anyway. He just gave me a much-needed push in the right direction, but I can see how it looks, and I hate that I've made you feel bad, baby. That's the last thing I want. I'm so sorry."

PJ shuffles down the couch and brushes his hand through my beard. "It's okay."

"You sure?"

He looks up at me with his mixed-colored eyes and nods. "I

believe you. Thank you for explaining everything and for not making me feel like even more of a fool than I am."

"You're not a fool. You had every right to be upset."

"I guess... I guess I still can't believe someone like you would even be remotely interested in—

"Finish that sentence..." I grab his wrist, easily enclosing it in my fingers. "And I will hit you."

PJ grins impishly. "Do I get to choose where?"

"Always, baby," I answer with a grin.

He nuzzles into my neck as I stroke his back. "But in all seriousness, I want you to know I'll never hurt you deliberately, PJ, and I'm going to do everything I can to make sure I don't hurt you undeliberately, either. Is that a real word? Undeliberately?"

He shrugs. "Let's go with it. I know what you mean."

"Are you really okay?"

"I am." He sits up again. "Is there anything else you haven't told me?"

"No. I swear. That was the only thing. Well, actually..."

"What?"

"There is one other thing I might not have mentioned."

"What?" he says again, slower this time.

"It's a little...awkward."

"Branum." His voice turns serious. "You can tell me anything. I won't judge you."

"Okay, well, in that case..." I try to suppress my smile. "I've always wanted to have sex in my office with a cute ginger, birdwatching geek. It's one of those bucket list things." I can't hold it in any longer, and a chuckle escapes out the corner of my mouth. "You know anyone that matches that description?"

PJ is on my lap as quick as lightning. "Actually, I do."

And with that, he kisses me, and we set about ticking that particular item off my bucket list.

16

PJ

"This is a big step," I announce on an exhale as Branum steers his pickup into the driveway of his oldest brother's cabin.

He parks and turns to face me. "You'll be fine, baby. My brothers can't wait to meet you."

It's been three weeks since we had sex in his office. After we came, Branum asked me to be his boyfriend, and I said yes. I also double-checked the following day in case he had inadvertently blurted the question out as part of his post-sex haze.

He hadn't.

We're together.

It's all very new, and we're both aware of that. We both also realize that, despite it being very, *very* early days in our relationship, what we have is real.

Which is why meeting his brothers is nerve-racking as hell but also something I'm excited about. I'm hoping this might also be a chance for me and Eddie to become friends, since lord knows I could do with some of those.

"Can I do anything? Are you *in balance*?"

I love when he asks me that, even though as I explained, and he understands, my OCD isn't a switch I can flick on and off. It's, unfortunately, not that predictable. But we agreed that it's still a good way for him to check in with me anyway.

"I'm okay. Nervous, but only because this means a lot to me."

He nods. "It's a pretty big deal for me, too. Never brought anyone home to meet the family."

"I'm the first?"

Branum smiles, threading his fingers through mine. "You're the first." He raises my hand to his mouth and kisses my palm tenderly. "And hopefully last."

My chest explodes with happiness. "For someone who doesn't see himself as a romantic guy, you're doing a pretty good job."

"That's because I've got a pretty good partner."

I give him a quick peck on the cheek and then we get out of the truck, both sporting huge smiles.

A man who looks like an older, less solid version of Branum opens the door and greets his brother with a hearty hug. When they break apart, Branum does the introductions. "PJ, this is my older brother, Marsh. Marsh, this is the one and only PJ."

He eyes me up and down, giving me the big brother once-over before bundling me up in a big hug, too. "Good to meet you, PJ."

"Same," I sputter, because the guy has a seriously strong grip.

Branum notices. "Hey, that's enough. You'll break him."

Marsh lets me go. "Sorry. Got a bit carried away."

"It's fine," I tell him, then turn to Branum and poke my finger into his chest. "And just so you know, it'll take a lot more than that to break me, mister."

I head inside, and as I do, I hear Marsh whisper, "I like him already."

It's nice catching up with Eddie again, and Harrick seems great, too. Such a talkative guy. The conversation flows easily between all of us right from the get-go.

Before I know it, there's a knock on the door.

"Food!" Branum exclaims, raising a triumphant fist in the air. "Thank god. I'm starving."

I chuckle as we make our way over to the dining room because we ate before we arrived. Branum really does have a big appetite. And not just when it comes to food. Hard to believe that up until three weeks ago, I was a virgin. These days, I've forgotten what it feels like to walk without feeling the after-effects of our lovemaking.

Not. Complaining. One. Bit.

We dig into the pizzas.

"Do you like your job at the library?" Harrick asks.

"I love it. I may be slightly biased, but people who love books are the best people. I really enjoy interacting with members of the community, and we do some fun activities, too."

"Such as?" Eddie asks.

"We run lessons for seniors teaching them how to use computers, and we host a weekly kids reading hour."

Branum glances my way, and I give him a small nod to say *I haven't forgotten.*

He and I have come up with a little plan, and considering Trevor owes me one, I'm pretty sure I'll be able to make it happen.

Once most of us finish eating, we retire to the den.

I sit next to Marsh, since Branum's cleaning the kitchen, which I think we all know is code for continuing to eat all the pizzas. I offered to help, but he gave me a kiss on the forehead and shooed me away. The bright twinkle in his eyes told me this night is going really well. I agree with him. It is.

I look at Marsh and smile. "So do you, um...have anyone?"

"No. I'm single."

"Oh. I'm surprised. You seem great."

"It's...*tricky*."

"You realize you saying that only makes me want to find out more."

He smiles a smile so strikingly similar to Branum's it makes me do a double take. "Let's just say I have some unconventional desires."

Part of me wants to find out what they are, but I don't want to make him uncomfortable. Plus, he's my boyfriend's brother, so there's probably a cap on how much I need to know about his love life and *unconventional desires.*

"Fair enough," I say, smiling diplomatically and trying to come up with another topic to move the conversation on to. "Are you into sports?"

"Smooth transition." He chuckles. "I like you, PJ."

"Thanks. I like you, too."

"And I like seeing my brother so happy. Both of them, actually."

Harrick and Eddie are canoodling on the other sofa.

I lower my voice. "You'll find someone. Hey, if I can, anyone can."

"Are you putting yourself down, baby?" Branum perches himself on the sofa arm. "Because we've discussed this, and if it turns out that you are, punishments will be involved."

"And that'd be my cue to leave."

Marsh gets up and Branum takes his place.

He returns with Monopoly, and the five of us spend the rest of the night wheeling and dealing and talking and laughing.

I can't remember the last time I had so much fun with a group of people.

Oh, wait, yes I can—Never.

This has turned into so much more than meeting Branum's brothers. It's turned into one of the best nights of my life.

As we start getting ready to leave, Harrick asks Branum, "How's your studying going?"

"Good," Branum replies. "I take the reading test in two weeks."

"Are you managing to cram in any studying?" Eddie asks.

Branum looks at me, his eyes intense with passion. "Oh yeah," he says with a sly grin. "Been doing lots of cramming."

17

Branum

The cramming is done.

Over.

I've spent the past few nights staying up way past my normal bedtime, trying to get—and keep—all the information in my brain.

I haven't done it alone, though. There was someone else right by my side the whole time, running over things with me, checking over my work, and fetching me snacks, which let's be honest, was probably the most important thing of all.

"Here we are," PJ announces as he parks my truck in the community college parking lot where the exam will take place. "How are you feeling?"

"How does anyone feel before an exam?"

"Good point." He leans over and cups my face in his delicate hands. "But you've done the work and are so well prepared. It'll go well."

"And if it doesn't?"

"Then we'll try again. And again. And again. For as long as we have to until you achieve your goal."

"Thank you so much, PJ. I couldn't have done this without you."

He smiles. "Yes, you could have. But honestly, I've enjoyed helping. You're the one doing all the work."

"I don't want to let you down."

"You won't. You can't. Even if you fail a million times, it doesn't matter. You're showing up and you're trying. *That's* the victory in all of this."

I blow out a breath. "You're right."

"I've got something for you."

"Ah, baby. You've already done so much. You didn't have to get me anything."

"I know." He grins widely. "But I wanted to."

"What is it?"

"Well..." He unbuckles his seat belt. "It's not a *thing*, as such. It's...this." He latches on to my shoulder, leans across the center console until he's by my ear, and whispers, "I love you."

I've only ever cried a handful of times in my life, but I swear, hearing those three words from him damn well nearly does me in.

"I love you, too. I've wanted to say it for a while, but I didn't want to scare you off."

"Scare me off?" He shakes his head, eyes glimmering. "I'm at your house every day. We spend all our free time together. And you fuck me senseless every night. You can't scare me off, because I am stronger than I look."

"You sure fucking are."

I sweep my boyfriend into my arms, and we start making out. I don't know how long we go at it for, but by the time we're done, the windows have fogged up.

"How am I going to be able to concentrate with *this*?" I run my hand over my bulging erection.

PJ giggles. "I can offer you an incentive."

"Oh yeah?"

"Yeah." His warm breath caresses my face. "I'll tell you what it is after the exam."

"No fair," I chuckle. "You're such a tease."

"True. I am. Now go in there, and ace that exam."

"How's this for an incentive?" PJ pants as I pound into his sweet hole.

"Pretty fucking good," I manage to grit out, holding his hips in place as I drive my cock into him.

We're meant to be birdwatching, not fucking on a boulder by the river... Oops. What can I say? Being in love is horny business.

Doesn't hurt that I got my test results back this morning.

I passed!

I can now officially read at a tenth-grade level. Next step, GED holder.

The sun is starting to fade, taking with it the warmth of the day. But we're getting close, so as soon as we're done, I'll take PJ back home...where we'll probably do this all over again.

"Getting clooose," he moans, reaching around for his dick.

"Same."

I'm holding on to his hips so tight I'm probably going to leave marks, but I like keeping him in place as I pummel into his channel.

He likes it, too, and with one final deep thrust from me, he cries out, and his whole body starts quaking as his release spills out.

Once he's done, I pull out. Without a word, PJ spins around, drops to his knees, and opens his mouth. He looks up at me, eyes sparkling, and murmurs, "Feed me."

Jesus. My legs buckle, but I give my baby what he wants. He laps up my release with his hungry mouth, and I crash down next to him.

"That was amazing," I say, finally catching my breath.

A lazy grin stretches his lips. "It always is. Come on."

He pushes to his feet and stretches out his arm.

"What are we doing?"

He glances at the river. "Let's go for a dip before it gets too cold."

"All right."

We dive into the cool blue water and frolic for a few minutes. We didn't bring towels so we dry off using our T-shirts. We pick up our stuff and head back toward my cabin.

"There you go, baby," I say, draping my jacket over PJ's shoulders.

He looks up at me and smiles, his wet red hair clumped to his face. "Thanks."

We walk hand in hand back to the house.

Life's a funny thing, isn't it?

I used to feel so lost. Not being able to read well does that to a person. It's a shameful secret I've carried my whole life. I've felt less than and scared that one day everyone will find out, and I'll be judged, laughed at, ridiculed.

But now look at me.

I can read, and I've found the most perfect man in the world.

The man I want to marry and, who knows, maybe have a ton of kids with one day.

The man I want by my side forever.

It won't be the most exciting life. No action-packed, city glitz here. But it will be a life filled with love. Reading. Birdwatching. Swims in the river and hikes through the mountains.

And love.

Nothing but my loyal, unwavering love for him. I'll never hurt him, and for as long as I draw breath, I'll do everything in my power to keep him safe.

Not because he needs protection, but because I truly believe that's what I was put on this earth to do—to treat my nerdy, ginger PJ like the king that he is.

18

PJ

"Are you sure he's not going to murder me with his bare hands?" Trevor whispers nervously beside me as the automatic doors pull apart and my sexy mountain man boyfriend strides in.

"He won't kill you with his bare hands," I assure my boss. "He'll most likely use his gun."

Trevor recoils in horror.

"I'm kidding. We've spoken about it, and he's okay with you. Really. Besides, you're doing him a favor. Relax. It'll be fine."

Yeah, it'll be fine *now*.

It took a lot of convincing on my part for Branum not to want to throttle Trevor anymore. The whole date-bet thing really was a silly misunderstanding. Branum gets fiercely protective of me, and I had to convince him Trevor's intentions weren't malicious, he just wanted to see us get together. It's all water under the bridge now.

Branum and I are together.

We're in love.

And that's all that counts.

Branum reaches the front counter and dips his head in greeting. "Trevor."

"Hi, how are you?" Trevor's voice comes out higher than normal. "*Greattoseeyouagain*!" He's also talking a million miles an hour.

My sexy mountain man appraises my boss for a moment before offering the poor bastard a friendly smile. "We're cool, man. I've got no one to blame but myself for not making a move on PJ sooner. I know you didn't mean anything malicious by saying what you did."

"So, I won't have my face plastered all over milk cartons as a missing person?"

Branum chuckles, extending his arm. "You won't."

They shake hands.

"And also," Branum adds. "Thank you for today. It's been something I've wanted to do since the first time I came here."

"Isn't that me?" I giggle, inserting myself cheekily into the conversation.

Branum chuckles. "It most definitely is. You're the first thing I wanted to do. This..." His eyes travel over the library. "Is the second."

"You wanna take him over?" Trevor asks me.

"Sure."

I step out from behind the counter and take Branum by the hand. "Your palm is sweaty," I whisper.

"Can you blame me?" he says back quietly.

"You'll be fine. The kids will love you."

"Sure hope so."

I give his clammy hand a squeeze as we approach the reading room. "You're going to be great."

"Thanks, baby." He looks down at me and smiles. "I love you."

"Love you, too. Now get in there before they turn feral."

"Yes, sir."

I follow him in, finding a spot in the back as Branum claps his hands together at the front of the room. "Hi, everyone! Who's ready for a story?"

A bunch of hands fly into the air.

"Me!"

"Me!"

"I ammmm!"

Branum smiles, and it lights up the whole room. "Good. I hope you like the book I've picked for you."

He sits his massive frame on a beanbag and begins reading. He takes his time, and I can hear the nervousness in his voice in the first few lines. After a few pages, he relaxes, and I smile. He's a natural at this.

My mind drifts, and I wonder whether one day Branum will be reading to *our* children.

How did I ever get so lucky?

I know that romances have to have a happily ever after, but this is something else.

He is something else.

It's rare to find a person who loves every part of you, even the bits that maybe you're not so keen on yourself.

Branum is that person for me. He sees everything—my unconventional appearance, my OCD, my geeky hobbies—and none of it makes him think twice about loving me with all his heart.

Just like I love him with all of mine.

I can't believe I get to spend the rest of my life with this incredible mountain man. This truly is the best happily ever after...ever!

~

Want more mountain man yummy-ness?

Flip the page for a sneak peek of The Reclusive Mountain Man!

SNEAK PEEK AT THE RECLUSIVE MOUNTAIN MAN

MARSH

Tal Bellamy is everything I'm not. A jet-setting playboy. A sexy silver fox. A guy who lives his life loudly and unapologetically.

We've been friends for almost twenty years. When he comes to town for a visit, I make a vow. There's something I need to get off my chest. Something I've been hiding.

Tal's the perfect guy to confide in because I know he won't judge me. The last thing I expect is to get plastered and hook up with him.

TAL

Marsh Duncan is a big, burly mountain man. A recluse. Grouchy at times. Or at least, that's what he wants people to think.

Not me. I know the man beneath the gruff exterior. When he's around his brothers or hanging out with me, his kindness and warmth shine through.

The truth is, Marsh is actually one giant marshmallow.

Another truth?... I'm all-out, head over heels, slap-me-sideways in love with him.

My plan is to confess my secret when I visit, not sleep with him. But it seems that I'm not the only one with something to reveal.

Now that we've both shared our truth, the question is: have we ruined our friendship, or are we on the brink of a forever love?

Chapter 1

Tal

"So who is this Marsh guy, and why are you flying to the other side of the planet to see him when you've just settled in here?" Rove asks me across the table.

"This fish is incredible," I say around a mouthful of barramundi. "Nothing beats freshly caught seafood, right?"

I stare out at the sun hovering above the horizon line and lighting up the sky with an ethereal pink and orange glow while Rove and Leo exchange a look. Leo's my best friend, Rove's his partner, and we're sitting on the bridge deck of my Riverra 78 Motor Yacht, which is berthed at their marina in North Queensland, Australia, a.k.a. my new home.

Yep, at the ripe old age of fifty-four, Tal Bellamy is finally ready to settle down.

Well, almost.

There's just one teeny tiny matter I need to take care of first.

"Marsh is a good friend of mine," I say.

Rove narrows his eyes. "Then how come you've never mentioned him before?"

"Because Tal's the king of compartmentalization," Leo answers for me.

He's right on the money, so I simply nod.

I have four distinct lives, in Florida, Palm Springs, Berlin, and London.

Or, *had*.

I'm entering into my consolidation era.

"That's actually come up in therapy," I tell them. "My therapist in Palm Springs has been encouraging me to explore why I feel the need to lead these separate lives."

Leo stops eating. "And what did you say to that?"

"I told her I'd be seeking a second opinion from my therapist in London."

Now, Leo knows me well enough to know I'm deflecting with an attempt at humor. Rove, on the other hand, looks like he doesn't know what to make of this conversation.

Or me.

I tend to get that a lot.

I'm almost fifty-five, and I'm the first to admit I can be a lot. Too much for most people to handle.

I think that's part of the reason why I've compartmentalized my life the way I have. I've always been a short burst guy. When I did athletics in high school, if I ran around the track, I came last. If I had to do a hundred-meter anything, I won the blue ribbon. I thrive on frenetic energy, and on some subconscious level, I suspect I never hang around in one place for too long so I don't outstay my welcome and get on people's nerves. Not everyone is the same as me, and I can be a lot.

"I've known Marsh for close to twenty years," I begin, leaving out the precise circumstances of how we met, since that's a story for another time. "He lives in a small mountain town in the US, and I pop in to visit him two or three times a year. We hang out and have fun. He's a great guy."

"I thought you didn't do repeats," Leo teases.

"We've never had sex."

Both of their mouths fall open. That also tends to happen a lot.

"H-how is that possible?" Leo manages to do something other than gape at me.

I could continue down this lighthearted banter path...or I could verbalize what's been going on in my head.

And my heart.

"Well...because I'm in love with him."

See, Rove's in a better position here. He never recovered after my first bombshell, so he remains frozen as is. Mouth open, nice and simple. Leo's face, on the other hand, has to restart the Tal Bellamy roller coaster of shock all over again. There's head shaking and bewilderment, culminating nicely in a crescendo of rapid blinking.

"How is *that* possible?" Rove speaks up. "I haven't known you forever like Leo, but I was under the impression you didn't do love. Or relationships. Or repeats."

He's absolutely right. I've never been cut out for relationships or marriage. I don't even like it when a guy spends the night.

"Maybe I'm growing up?" I offer. "Maybe buying a yacht is the first phase of my new life where I settle down, hang up my G-strings, and start wearing more sensible underwear."

"Now *that part* I can definitely get on board with," Leo mutters to Rove, who shakes his head vigorously.

Hey, if you were in your fifties and had a sublime ass without a hint of cellulite, wouldn't you be showing it off, too?

"But seriously," I continue. "I've been doing a lot of reflecting lately. I've reached a point in my life where it's safe to say I've done everything I set out to. I have a successful career. I'm set up financially. I've fucked *allll* the twinks in Berlin. I... I want something else. Something like what you guys have. You know, love and all that shit."

They're both quiet for a while. I get it. It's a big shock.

Leo and I have been friends for over thirty years. He knows

me better than anyone, so he especially knows that I have never once even mentioned wanting to be in a relationship...or dropped the L-bomb.

"What's he like?" Leo asks, breaking the silence. "He must be pretty fantastic if he's got you like this."

"He's... He's..." I smile.

"Uh-oh," Rove says, nudging Leo with his elbow. "Looks like Tal's got it bad."

I nod. "Yeah. I think I do. Marsh is nothing like my usual type when it comes to sex."

"Twinks with daddy issues?" Leo and Rove guess at the same time.

Okay, so I have a type. Sue me.

"Exactly."

"How old is he?"

"Forty-one."

"Whoa," they say in unison.

"He's a mountain man. Rugged and masculine. Deep voice. Wears flannel. Chops wood. The whole thing."

My smile grows bigger and bigger as my mind fills with the image of Marsh chopping wood. Seriously, it's like a porn scene come to life.

"So not who I pictured you falling for." Leo sounds shocked.

"That makes two of us, but I've been looking into this love thing. Apparently it's a lot of things but logical isn't one of them."

They nod their heads in agreement.

"Love is a decision, not just a feeling," Leo says, smiling at me as he repeats the words I once uttered to him when he and Rove were figuring their stuff out in the early days of their relationship.

"Yeah. It's that, too."

"And this Marsh guy, ya reckon he's the one?" Rove asks, his Aussie accent coming through strong.

"I don't know." I blow out a breath, glancing between them. "That's why I'm flying over next week to visit him."

"What are you going to do when you get there?" Leo asks.

"I'm going to tell my friend I'm in love with him and pray like hell that it doesn't fuck up our nearly twenty-year friendship."

Get the book on Amazon now!

ABOUT CASEY COX

Casey Cox is an Australian MM romance author whose work includes the hugely popular *VET SHOP BOYS* series.

Casey loves spending time at the beach and is the proud paw-rent to two utterly adorable French Bulldogs - Ralphie and Lilly.

For more information about Casey, please visit -
www.caseycoxbooks.com

Printed in Great Britain
by Amazon